One NRI Girl

One NRI Girl

This book is dedicated to all women.

Introduction

Sonja is a divorced and attractive Indian girl. She is working as a software engineer in an investment bank in USA. She has money ($$$$), she can afford sex outside marriage. She also has opinion on everything. She is dating various marriage prospects, will she get her dream guy?

One NRI Girl I

Mr. Adams, director in a Chinese Multinational based BPO called me and said, "I have already fallen in love with you, gorgeous! Your black eyes are deep enough to crush my heart. Do not say NO, I want to meet you this weekend."

I said "Sorry" out of reflex - a shy attempt to a refuse for a harsh-of-a-man to me. I was expecting a more persuasive approach, like at least he should have tried to convince me. It felt more like a DEMAND.
"I will drive out of Boston to meet you, and I will pick you up from your home, then take you to a good restaurant for dinner." he insisted.
Like that promise is all the romanticism he could ever give.

The director picked me from my home and gave me a very firm handshake

while starring in my eyes, with a
medieval grin on his face.

"How are you doing sweet girl?" He
asked in a cheerful voice.
His perfume overloading the
surroundings, pushing me once again
into regrets for this date. Makes me
believe that is all he has to offer was a
single wish.
His hands were coarse, while shaking
hand; he started ogling at my breast,
my breath was pushing my bra to its
limits.
I had to apply little bit of force to take
my hand out of his clutch.

"I have already fallen in love with you,
you are the light I searched for so
many years, Sonja can't you see?
What is joy if you are not with me; I

would not wish any companion in the
world but you. "

(My Impressions)
"Companion"!? Like his little pet,
beloved and caged.
I asked, "How could you fall in love
even before meeting me?"

He said, "I looked at your profile photo
for an hour, you look so gorgeous,
your eyes look like a rare black
diamond. I need the shine of your
diamond eyes when evening descends
in my life. You came in my sweet
dream, kissed me, hugged me and
then we made love, it was best dream
I have ever had, Sonja."
AND SHOULD STAY SO!

"Stop lying, shut up!" I diverted topic, "What was reason for your divorce?" He slapped his forehead and said, "My ex wife was 2 months pregnant at our first night."

While driving, he was trying to rub his leg with mine, I just moved away a little bit.

"We are going to have dinner at China Minar", He insisted.

"Please have some vodka, we will be able to converse more freely then." I politely refused. He took few glasses of Vodka and told me, "Sonja darling, I want to marry you, can I get a hug from you?"

My best friend Michelle had warned me about this tactics used by the guys at

first date, if hug request is accepted -
they grab the girl and kiss on the lips,
then grope everywhere. I rejected his
hug request. He drank few more
glasses of vodka. Suddenly He
pleaded, "I will not be able to drive
home, can you take me to the nearest
hotel?"
I CALLED A CAB AND GOT HIM INTO
IT.
Thanks to the gentile waiter for the
effort of truly listening to me.

I left the restaurant alone into the cold
autumn night. It was a silent walk
under the sole whispers of my
wondering dreams.... of love. Will I
ever get my true love? Few drop of
tears started rolling down my cheek.

MOTTO: "Solitude is fine but you need someone to tell that solitude is fine." - Honore de Balzac.

Next day, I got a call from Mr. Adams that he drove back to Boston and he would make me repent my decision. I just disconnected the call, he again called back. I again disconnected and phoned right away to my best friend Michelle for advice. She advised, "Just accept the phone and then keep the phone inside your vanity bag." I used this trick to get rid of the director from my life.

One NRI Girl II

One of my college class mate found me in dating website and expressed his acute interest in me.

Chris came to my flat to meet me; It was intriguing even for me how did I invited him TO MY FLAT! But I was quite comfortable with him from college days and had to feed my vanity a little bit: by having him see my financial success and lifestyle.

"You were the heart throb of all our boys in college. At college, I was heavily infatuated with you, but as you were the most beautiful and arrogant girl, I could not gather the courage to propose you, I used to think about you a lot, you used to meet me in my dream, behind your back, we used to call you 'Sexy Sonja'", he laughed like a child.

"Shut up!" I said pretending to be angry, enjoying his memories.

"Cool down dear, here is a song for you," as Chris start to recite I open a bottle of red wine.

"I wrote Sonja in the sky,
but the wind removed it.
I wrote Sonja in the sand,
but the waves removed it.
I wrote Sonja in my heart,
and nothing can remove it.

As we start to taste the sweet wine,
Chris start to warm up.

"I still love you Sonja, always did! By the way, why did you get divorced, your hubby could not tolerate your arrogance?" he asked.

I yelled at him, "Shut up, you can't even imagine! My husband had a mistress who got pregnant after our marriage and had the guts to request me to get out of his lover's life."

"I am sorry, Sonja, I should not have joked about your divorce." he told looking at my eyes.

"It's Ok, I would have dump him anyway. What's your story?" I asked back stretching a bit on the comfortable sofa we sat. I could not help to notice how he got his eyes stalked on my hornet waist -

suffocated with a tight leather belt
over my short dress.

He said, "It is somewhat similar,
before our marriage, my ex wife was in
love with a non Christian, who made
her pregnant and then told that, she
has to convert and change life style
completely as per his religion".
"Did she?" I asked curiously.
Chris served us more wine as he
caught my interest, FINALLY.
"Luckily, her parents were against her
converting to a new religion. Therefore
her sectant lover said that his religion
does not allow marrying with an
outsider, neither provide heritage a
child in any financial or spiritual ways."
Chris remembers with obvious heart
nausea, taking a deep breath before
continuing:

"My ex-wife was forced to do an abortion and so she developed a strong guilt, considering that she has killed her own baby. Her parents found an idiot in me marry her."

MY MOOD SUDDENLY CHANGED INTO THE START OF A DEPRESSION AS I TRIED TO PICTURE MYSELF IN THAT POSITION.

I could only sob to him: "Really? How did you get persuaded by her parents to marry her"?

Chris recalls without any sign of remorse, "Her father was the CEO of my workplace; I got promoted with a huge boost in my income. On top of that I was shareholder in her dad's company."

I could not refrain myself into asking him: "You are into a pretty bad shape now Chris, how did you end up this way?"

He continued, "Few days after marriage, she told me about her past and begged me for a kid, we tried for 3 months without any luck and then went to see a doctor, the doctor diagnosed both of us for infection and gave us some cream and tablets. Her abortion had indeed caused serious infection issue and I got same infection from her. 3 more months passed by and one fine morning, my ex wife started to have pregnancy symptoms, I got delighted, got pregnancy test kit and it tested positive. I was feeling elated. Then her parents came and told that it would be better that she stays in her parent's house, my wife delivered a baby boy, then suddenly her ex boyfriend started meeting her.

"REALLY?" I popped up interrupting him.

Bowing his head in shame, Chris shared the outcome of his story, "Her sextant lover had some sex tapes with my wife. As he demanded a six digit sum to her father I have refused the payment and so I got kicked out of her life by her parents. The same parents who got me into it."

MY MOOD CHANGED AGAIN FROM SLOWLY DEPRESSED INTO COMPASSION FOR THE POOR GUY. "Forget it Chris, it has passed. Forget that experience!"
He exclaimed "That is not all!" And I thought "Oh my GOD, what's next!?"

Chris explained in detail how that sextant lover sold the sex tapes to porn sites and his wife went into a severe depression, giving birth prematurely and going into mental hospital while his son is raised by the grandparents who kicked him out of their life and company. Blaming Chris for refusing the payment for the blackmail that now went BOOM. Leaving him completely broke".

I thought to myself "Pretty bad, we could have made a good couple, but I can help him back on his feet."

"WOULD YOU STILL MARRY ME, SONJA?" he asked again.

"Chris, I need 6 months time to decide about your marriage proposal"

I told only half the truth as I am
expecting to keep him in the fridge for
6 months, if I do not get any better
match, I will settle for him, IF he gets
back on his feet. We have interacted
with each other for 4 years in college,
he was a descent and helpful person,
he was not a womanizer, and he may
be a good match for me."

"Fine Sonja, I'll wait!" And he starts to
sing again.

O how many times may the moon-
shine reflected in your black eyes?
Should it be that we can hear,
the woes of those who broke their
lives?
As I fell asleep I barely heard his
"Good Night, Sonja".

The next morning I found coffee and breakfast with a farewell note and him gone. I thought about Chris's experience just as

Motto: "Where there is love there is life." -Mahatma Gandhi

One NRI Girl III

Mr. Bronson, a Bank manager, invited me for dinner after seeing my profile on the dating website.

I was very worried that day, as credit recovery unit called me and told that they would break my fixed deposit to recover pending credit card amount. So I took the Banker's meeting as a good sign for my misfortune.

Mr. Banker took me to a cheap restaurant, He asked, "You seem to be quite worried, can I help in some way?" I said, "I am getting harassed by credit card department, I had requested bank to close my credit card two years back, I do not have any proof of that, now they send me a new credit card with a a call from credit card agency that I need to pay them $5000 to clear my credit card dues. I tried to convince them that I have closed my credit card long back, they asked me to send proof of closure, I could not find it, now they are saying they will break my fixed deposit, which has got nothing to do with the credit card issue."

His face shine upon my subject in his best fields of interest: banking.
"Well, never deal with bank informally, you could have sent an email to close the credit card and when they

responded with credit card closure statement, you could have saved those emails in your mailbox. You did a big mistake and there is not much to do about this. It is a standard trick played by the banking goons." Seeing me very worried he got into the marriage subject.

"How many guys have you seen so far?"
"In my case, not many people are interested to marry a divorced, independent and proud woman. I have dated around 10 guys so far," I replied.

I wondered if his tactic was to get in my pants or to reach to my heart and challenged him a bit. "I need some more advices from you, my mortgage EMI is going up every few month, and what can I do to reduce it?"

He answered, "Well, you can take a loan from your 401/life insurance at cheap rate and prepay lump sum amount of your mortgage."

"You are a genius, Thanks Mr. Bronson," I exclaimed.

"Sonja, I think I have already fallen in love with you" and he quoted an anonymous lover:
"Meeting you was fate, becoming your friend was a choice, but falling in love with you I had no control over."

Ten years older than me, sort of a geek style with a common face and a humble attitude. Not exactly my type. "I would not mind spending my life with you, but I need six more months to decide, we can meet few more times," I tried to keep him in my deep freeze as an option.

"I know that I am 10 years older than you, but I am quite active sexually, I will not give you any chance to complain. Of course you can take your time; I will be waiting for you dear," He told in a romantic tone.

He drove me back to my flat and played few romantic songs while driving back. I told him I like "Always" from Bon Jovi and he replied, "That's one of my favorite also. See? our taste for music is similar, we will make a good couple."

"Hopefully," I murmured.

"Do you know why lovers call each other Honey?" he asked.

I answered in negative.

He quoted, Victor Hugo,

"Life is a flower of which love is the honey."

"That is good to know!" I exclaimed.

He neither tried to touch me inappropriately, nor did he insist for sex, he seems to be my man, but he is 10 years older than me. I thought, "Now I have got at least two person in hand, let me search for six more months, if I do not find anyone better than Bronson, I will marry him." I thanked my luck for helping me find a life partner.

But as usual, destiny had different plan for me. I asked Michele to run a background check on Mr. Bronson. My friend used her network to find out that Mr. Bronson already have one son from his first marriage. I found the idea that "my children would have to share property with his son" unpalatable, since Mr. Banker hide the detail about his son from first marriage it was another good reason to cut him from my list.

Motto: "Anything is better than lies and deceit!" -Leo Tolstoy

One NRI Girl IV

Mr Allen, an IT professional accepted my dating proposal.

He came to my house in an afternoon and took me to nearest restaurant by cheap cab.

In the cab, he asked, "What perfume do you use? It smells awesome."

He quoted George Moore,

"The hours I spend with you I look upon as sort of a perfumed garden, a dim twilight, and a fountain singing to it. You and you alone make me feel that I am alive. Other men it is said have seen angels, but I have seen thee and thou art enough."

I told, "I am using some ordinary deodorant and you must be flattering!" "No, I really mean it," he told in a serious tone.

Suddenly, He saw one butterfly chasing another nice looking butterfly. He said, "Look Sonja, even these two butterflies are out in a date today, very much like us." He quoted John Keats,

"I almost wish we were butterflies and lived but three summer days - three such days with you I could fill with more delight than fifty common years could ever contain."

We reached the restaurant before Mr. Allen could quote any more poetry, We ordered the "Menu of the day" and stood together to eat, he started asking intimate questions, crowd in the restaurant were looking at us, they started laughing by hearing his dialogues. He then told, "Sonja, I would like to date you 12 times before deciding to marry." He then wrote down his food expense.

Suddenly, he got a call from a girl, he got much tensed, and he told in the phone, "I am in a meeting with my clients. Please call me after an hour." I could hear all of the conversation, as the girl was shouting at top of her voice and was addressing the guy as darling. When, I asked about the call, he said, "A girl from my hometown is very interested to marry me, I have already communicated that our status does not match. Still, she is heckling me."

I thought, "Allen is really a cheap guy who is dating girls for some extra fun, while having a stable girl friend at hometown."

He dropped me back to my home by an auto rickshaw.

We met again, this time; we walked down for a mile in the evening breeze to go to the nearby eatery. "Sonja, we should stop taking cab for small distance and rather walk hand in hand in evening, it feels so romantic," He exclaimed. Again we ordered "menu of the day", after few minutes, same girl called him. Mr Allen talked to her tensely for few minutes and said, "I am in traffic, I will call you back in an hour." The girl shouted from the other side of the phone, "Sweetheart, why are you trying to avoid me now? I gave you everything, you promised me to marry immediately after getting a job, now it is almost six months and you are just avoiding me, if you do not marry me, I will commit suicide and you will be held responsible for my death, everybody knows in our hometown that we slept with each other, now you cannot refuse me, you have to marry me!"

I listened to the conversation and pretended not to hear anything. He smiled with unease and said, "You know this country girls, the moment one gets a good job, they start heckling for marriage." "Sonja, we already dated twice, can we go to love park for few hugs and kisses, the bush in the park provides complete privacy," he enquired looking at my eye. I told, "I am not interested in all that before marriage, I need to leave," We came out from the eatery, I called a cab, he advised, "Sonja darling, just walk down to your flat, you can save few bucks for the future." I thought, "This guy is a cheap miser who wants to have fun and then ditch girls after sleeping with them."

I blocked him in my dating profile; he immediately called me asking reason. I said, "You are not serious about marriage, I have overheard your conversation with that girl, stop fooling girls like that."

MOTTO: "Cheating and lying aren't struggles; they're reasons to break up."- Patti Callahan Henry.

One NRI Girl V

Mr. Gallagher, HR Manager of a large IT company called me and said, "We need to know each other better and decide whether we can spend rest of

our life together, let's meet for dinner
tonight."

He took me to one of costliest hotel "La
Palace" for a dinner.

"Sonja, I wrote poetry about you," he
recited,

My heart and soul is thirsty for Sonja's
love,
A sweet princess whom world has not
maligned yet,
A sweet princess to love and to
protect.
A vow to myself I make,
As she quietly sleeps away;
To love and always cherish Sonja,
Until my last breath
Until my last day.

I said, "I loved it, but this poetry is written by Michael Brieck, not you!" He smiled with little embarrassment and kept quiet for some time after which he asked, "Sweet girl, can I kiss your hand?"

"Yes." He immediately kissed my right hand and licked it once before leaving the hand and then commented, "Your hand is sweeter than sugar!" I sensed not only his eagerness to perverse fantasies but also an evident awkwardness specific to mid age bold, fat and rich managers. To change topic, I told, "You are managing human resource of such a huge company, is it a very challenging job?" while we lose ourselves on the evening boulevard that leads to "La Palace".

"Not exactly, it is easier to manage employees due to large number, anyone who comes to complain, we have got a set of standard answers, 1. 'Read policies', 2. 'Everyone else is happy, we cannot change policy for you alone'. 3. 'You are violating policies which can result in disciplinary action up to termination', etc." he continued boasting his HR management skills.

We got into "La Palace" a Victorian stylish restaurant with lots of good taste paintings and comfortable atmosphere for every Wall Street wannabe in town, serving a tea with brown sugar cubes. Not my cup of tea I must admit. Sitting on a reserved table cornered by romantic blue lights, saxophone and jazz brakes the silence. Suddenly Mr. Gallagher revives himself, bringing back his preferred topic: how good he is into HR Managing.

He chuckled, offering me some brown sugar for my tea. "No thanks, I am coffee addicted" I said - A gentle refusal.

"We have got 50 pages of policy book, employees are supposed to read, understand and sign it at the time of joining. We have rigorous policies and we fine employees for violating of policies, we even terminate them for violating any policy."

I asked, "Any example?"

"Like, if people are not wearing tie/formal shoes, we fine them USD 100, if people take more than 10 minutes bathroom break, we fine them

USD 100 more, we have installed swipe machine in each of our bathroom and hope to recover the cost of installation in 5 years."

As the conversation freeze so does my coffee. I try to close on him the smart way. I quipped, "Your department should be renamed to 'HRH' in lieu of 'HRD', 'Human resource harassment' in lieu of 'Human resource development'. You are driving a Mercedes and brought me to costliest hotel, does HR earn huge salary in your company?" I asked.

He replied, "Not exactly, we have underhand deals with job consultants, we are supposed to pay one month salary to them when we hire a candidate referred by them, so we get a 25% cut from all referrals, we get it in cash!"

"I am planning to apply to your company, can you please refer me? I pleaded"

"No, most of the IT managers are big bastards, they will sleep with you, by hook or crook, I do not want to bear burden of some other bastard's child for whole of my life!, Please try in non IT companies."

We stood confident and silent for the rest of the evening. My coffee arrived. It was not an extraordinary one given the Victorian standards I have. "Thanks Mr. Gallagher, for the information and for the coffee, but I think that we are not physically compatible. I am sorry," I told in a soft tone.

There was silence for few moments. Mr HR Manager scratched his bald head and took a deep breath, "Ok, I will drop you to your house," it was all he could say.

MOTTO: Marilyn Monroe: "A sex symbol becomes a thing. I hate being a thing."

He drove me back; he did not speak at all. Once I came out of the car, I said, "Thanks, Good night." He bade good night and vanished from my life forever.

One NRI Girl VI

I accepted 'dating interest' of Mr.
Dunja, a self proclaimed libertine. We
met for dinner in a costly restaurant.

"You are Sonja, I am Dunja, our name
rhymes well, we will make a good
couple" he introduced himself.
"What have names got to do? We can
call rose with any name we want yet
its fragrance still enthuses the
passerby" I quipped smilingly.
"You have got very beautiful smile
Sonja, being blessed with sensual lips
that underline well your uplifting
cheeks. Do not ever lose your smile!"
he tried to complement me.
"If I could reach up and hold a star for
every time I smile, the entire evening
sky would be in the palm of my hand."
I replied ironically and cut it short to

see his reaction: "Let's stop the complements and order some food, I'm starving.

He quoted Plato: "At the touch of love everyone becomes hungry" and insisted "Sonja for our love's sake, let's get a digestive before dinner, you will feel yourself more relaxed, with all your appetite unleashed" I refused any alcohol, Michelle warned me to avoid drinking and be rational at any first date.
He drank two glasses of vodka and started talking nonsense, with stupid affirmations such "I dislike independent girls" and giving hints for a "first date sex". So far this guy has been the most direct of all.

"There are many girls who refuse things like one night stand - sex at first date, giving nonsense reason like culture, religion, family and principles. I tell them, If you have sex with condom on, there is really no risk or consequence, worst case, you may have to take a morning after pill so why would you deprive yourself from sexual enjoyment? Many married women told me that it is quite boring to have sex with the same partner year after year that is why today's trend to share partners and get out of the boredom."

I asked, "What kind of relationship should people have in an ideal libertine world? He replied "Ideally, any one should be able to have sex with any number of partners they wish."

SUDDENLY I GOT A SENSATION OF SICKNESS.

"That is quite... animalist. Inhuman since there is not much of a feeling involved," I replied.

He argued "Look at the main problems depicted in almost all movies, you will find the following pattern, Ms X is in love with Mr Y, she loves Mr Z and have had physical relationship with Mr W, now Mr Z is married to Ms A, who was ex wife of Mr W, they meet each other, curse, crib and have sex"
A satisfactory smile got onto my face and took away my hunger sensation for a moment.
"It is quite a retarded comparison. Movie scripts are all that you can argue with?"

He again started talking nonsense, "In the animal reign, there is absolute sexual freedom, no need to buy consent for sex, no child support, no divorce, no molestation, no rape cases. Libertines are fighting to free the human kingdom from all kind of sexual prejudices. We dream of a day, where any guy can have sex with any girl and legalize prostitution in every country following the Dutch example."

Another bad example I thought and served him a little bit of logic: "There are many differences between animals and humans like ability to control passion, compassion, love, kindness, conscience, dependence and so on. How will returning the humankind back to animal reign will liberate the society? That is an obvious regression, NOT evolution"

His last argument was "You do not understand how much animals enjoys their life without any law, prejudices and fear of consequences!" and I could not refrain myself from asking "What about pedophilia, zoophilia, etc.?" Those are not happening in the animal reign and therefore my opinion is that should not be allowed in my kind of society"

I got really fed up with his libertine views. I finished up my dinner quickly and told him that I would like to leave, not before asking his age.

"23 and very potent" he proudly stated.
He screamed, "What, I want to spend whole night with you and you want to leave now, are you one of the girls, who just loots guy and get away without paying anything back, I spent $100 for your dinner, is it not enough,

am I not good enough for you? I bet,
you will love by performance in bed.
Let's rent one of the restaurant's room,
I promise, you will enjoy my
company."

"Grow up and get a life" was the only
advice I could give. I took my bag and
tried to leave, he grabbed my hand
and pleaded me not to leave, I told
him in calmly "Leave my hand, or else
I will scream and create a scene."
Trying to hurt my feelings the poor guy
mumbled "You should stop dating
guys, if you are not interested in sex
after dinner, stop wasting our money!"

He did not deserve a farewell. He is so
far my worse dating experience.

MOTTO:

"Young age can be experience just once, but immaturity never leaves even when we grow up" -Steve Jobs.

One NRI Girl VII

Mr. Roland, a company promoter accepted my 'dating interest'. We met for dinner at a nearby restaurant. He introduced himself in style, "Hi, I am Roland, doing my PhD." I am researching on a very interesting subject, "How IT Service Company can become increasingly efficient and exponentially profitable". He smiled and started bragging, "I own large stakes in 2 IT service companies, second company is a premium one and charges 25% more than average to the clients. For the first company we charge 25% less than average market.

Clients looking to reduce their cost offer us projects to first company and clients looking for quality gives projects to second company. Internally, first company gives part of the project to our second company, that way we make profit whether clients want to cut cost or they are ready to pay more for quality." I asked, "How do you make company, increasingly efficient and exponentially profitable?" trying to look interested on the matter.

"Simple, we are into IT service business; we hire thousands of people from colleges and then train them in particular technologies in order to send them on work for the client's projects. They work for 12-15 hours including Saturday and Sunday. When a project gets closed, we ask our trainees to search for a new client on their own within a month, if they find it- their job is safe, else we lay them off and we even hesitate to pay lay off compensation. This way we get free work and more new projects."

I said, "That's horrible and unscrupulous exploitation, will not employees sue you?"

He grinned with satisfaction and explained, "No chance, government, judges, lawyers, politicians, mobsters have invested a lot in shares at our company. We can also send a few scary faces to bully the ex employee and withdraw his case against us." He chuckled.

I thought to myself for a moment to RIP OFF this sadistic financial psycho.

He said with lot of conviction, "I would like to make my companies as profitable as Google. At Google, 3000 odd people are generating 10 billion dollar profit. Our company is only making 10 million dollar profit with 6000 engineers."

It was a good moment to attack his ego and so I did!
"Your company can only steal other works, never compete with Google. Your engineers may be just searching for code in Google and copying it into your projects, but sooner or later your company's IP addresses will be banned and you will fail to deliver projects with stolen codes." He suddenly changed the subject.

"Do you know the concepts of Flower Power dating, like partner swap as in the mid 60s Silicon Valley?"

"Like sex, drugs and rock 'n' roll?" I asked disgruntled. He replies fast "I am fed of all that, I want a family to pass on my legacy. Will you marry me, sweet girl?"

I asked, "If you are fed up with sex, why do you want to marry?" and the reply came just as I expected: "To make a family, I got so much wealth, I need to pass the wealth down to the next generation of Roland. I promise you to take to Switzerland for honeymoon. I will also transfer one percentage of my shares in your name," he grabbed my right hand and said, "Will you marry me, sweet girl?"

"Yes Sir, who can refuse a billionaire!"
I replied.

He said, "That's great. Can we live in for a month just to understand our physical and mental compatibility? If we do not find each other compatible we can part away as friends and I will give you 1000 company shares as a gift."

I asked for time and left the restaurant, I called up my best friend Michelle to know her opinion about Mr. Roland.

She started screaming over the phone, "Roland is a playboy, he gets into brief relationships with a new girl every month, and makes them perform like porn star. If the girl fails to perform well, Roland abuses her physically, threatens her to fire from the 'dream life". Once his lust gets satisfied, he dumps her and gives 1000 shares, most of the girl runs away from him in one or two days, he has got few million shares, he can continue to live in with a new girl every month till the end of his life." I asked Michelle, "How do you know?" and she replied mysteriously, "Let's meet this Sunday for lunch; I will share more details about that bastard!"

Mr. Roland called me after a week and asked, "What did you decide honey?" At that moment I was very close for a GO with the sole purpose of ruining him but I realized this is not my goal. I only disconnected the call.

Motto:

The man who has won millions at the cost of his conscience is a failure. - B.C. Forbes

One NRI Girl VIII

Mr. Sherman, a pharmacy professional came in his stylish bike and took me to nearby restaurant for dinner.

Every now and then, he was putting brakes on his bike unnecessarily, my breasts were touching his back and he was making low noise in joy. I then put my bag in front of my breasts, from next time, only my bag started touching his back. He told in an angry voice, "Why did you do that Sonja? Did you not like it?"

I just kept quiet. We reached the restaurant in 15 minutes.

He came in a sleeveless shirt; every now and then he was lifting his hands over his head for showing his biceps, exposing ugly hairs in his armpits. He said, "Girls get aroused by looking at my biceps. Do you like them?"

Every time he was lifting hand above head, some bad smell was coming from his arm pits. I said, "Please stop showing your muscles!"
"You know Sonja, I have had 5 love affairs so far, I have roamed around in my bullet with dozens of girls, but I could only have physical relationship with 5 girls, so far, me being a body builder, I feel that I am quite unsuccessful getting laid. Can you please suggest me few tips on how to increase my chance to get laid," he whined.

I replied, "You may shave your armpit and use some perfume for the start!"

"That's one idea, I will try this with my next date," He exclaimed.

I intervened "It's much easier for a girl to find a partner, than for a man".

He continued pretending he hasn't heard my line "I would like to date you at least 6 times; you look so hot and unexplored! We can take sex steroids tonight and have marathon sex for hours; you will feel that, you are in heaven for that period of time. I brought, morning after pill; you can take one tomorrow morning, no need to fear for pregnancy."

I said, "Mr Sherman, we are not compatible."

He whispered, "We will become compatible after having sex 108 times as prescribed in Kamasutra, you will love it so much that you will not be able to stay without sex even for a day."

"Are you really so dumb or acting like dumb, I do not want to sleep with dumb guy like you, get lost," I screamed again.

"Ok, then please refund me the $150 that I have spent with hope of having sex with you, since you are not interested, I am entitled for a refund," he said.

"I gave you advice on how to make yourself more attractive to girls, the cost of that was exactly $150, now get lost," I told in soft tone.

"Ok, can I drop you back to home, I can at least get some boob bumps," he said.

I went out of the restaurant straight away and took a cab to come back to my flat.

MOTTO: "Huge biceps are an unattractive-uneducated-underpaid man's last attempt to be seen as worthy of dating, or, sleeping with."- Mokokoma Mokhonoana.

One NRI Girl IX

Mr. Nelson, a business analyst, picked me from my home in his car.

While driving, he started looking at my shaved arm pit every now and then; I could even see his tongue coming out few times, most likely he was thinking of licking me from my abdomen till my arm pit.

Then he focused on my breasts, he started showing his teeth, most likely he was thinking about biting them.

He said, "Sonja, I have bought a surprise gift for you." He took out a pink panty from his bag. I refused to take the gift.

He asked, "What color are you wearing now, what color do you like? I will exchange it and bring it at next date"

I screamed, "Shut up!"

"Do you watch porn?" he inquired looking at my eye.

"Occasionally," I told.

He said, "What kind of porn do you watch? I got 12 GB porn collections; I spend hours watching them every day. Watching porn is so liberating experience for me; I love rape porn very much. After dinner, let's go to my place, I will show you many porn videos, you will love it.i"

I said, "Watching porn regularly rewires brain to think women as sex object only, you are already addicted to porn, do you ever plan to come out of this addiction?i"
He replied, "All men think women as sex object only, but since women do not like that, men lie to women and

wrap their lust with a rose or perfume or dinner or a trip, These are simple tricks to trap women and make them sleep with us! The girls are so stupid that they fall for this trick again and again, my guess is, even women have become like men now, they just want good food, good car, good wine and in exchange of that, they are ready to sleep with any guy."

I said, "You are a total pervert and a lost case." He told, "I have learnt by experience, that whole world is held together due to sexual intercourse, if all women refuse to have sex for a month, their men will start killing each other in anger and frustration, without sex, all men will go mad in a month. So I am perfectly normal guy."

I got a call from Michelle; I just came out of the dining hall to take the call. When I went back to the table he offered me a soft drink. He might have mixed some drugs in my drink, I started feeling very unwell. He told, "You need to take some rest," I was semi conscious; He took me to a room adjacent to the dining hall, which he seemed to have rented in advance. Michelle called me again, I told her, "I am at 'Restaurant Hellfire' with Nelson, I am feeling very unwell, I may lose consciousness any time, please come and save me."

Mr Nelson threw me into bed, and undressed within a minute and lied on top of me and started sucking my lip, he squeezed my breasts, and his tool started hurting my private part. I asked him to stop it, he laughed and said, "Relax darling, please cooperate with me, you will enjoy, I will have fun for some time and drop you back to your home."

I thought he might rape me any time, but I was unable to put up any fight, my muscles were getting cramped.

15 minutes passed by, I almost lost consciousness and door bell rang, Nelson put a bed sheet on top of my naked body and went to answer the door bell.
Michelle, along with her boyfriend and another friend barged into the room, they caught my aggressor by collar, slapped him, while Michelle's boyfriend gave a kick to Nelson as he run away from the room. They chase and caught him, delivering him to the manager of the restaurant. In the mean time,

Michelle dressed me back. The manager refused to call police and said, "Both might have taken sex drugs consensually and your friend passed out due to over dose, police will even arrest her, she would have to undergo drug test, she will get into trouble in her career and social life. Rape did not happen, Please sort it out outside our restaurant."

Michelle and her friends carried me to the car and got myself admitted to nearby hospital. They gave me 3 bottles of saline; I regained complete consciousness in around two hour. I thanked Michelle and her friends from the bottom of my heart for saving me from getting raped.

I complained about Nelson's profile in the dating website, they just banned his user id.

MOTTO: "By living a life to harm others," the deviant or pervert becomes a hero or heroine in decadent fiction."- Asti Hustvedt.

One NRI Girl X

Mr. Stampler, a project lead working in a large Silicon Valley Corporation, asked me to meet at "Coffee House" in downton by 7PM. As there was heavy traffic, I got delayed by 15 minutes. The moment, I arrived at "Coffee House", I found an awesome looking guy waiting impatiently and checking his watch frequently, I went near him and said,

"Hi Mr. Stampler, I am Sonja, How are you doing?" He shook hand softly and gave me a smile, saying, "You are late by 15 minutes, are you late by habit?" "No, there was a huge traffic jam near 5th Avenue," I said.

"Sonja, you are extremely beautiful and do not have much pride with your beauty, I like your humbleness and I am searching for a girl like you! I feel I have already fallen in love with you, Sonja! Do you have any remedy for Love?"

"There is no remedy for love but to love more. "I blushed, quoting Thoreau.

He quoted back from the Bible - Corinthians 13:13: "And now these three remain: faith, hope and love. But the greatest of these is love."

We all want to fall in love. Why?
Because that experience makes us feel
completely alive. Where every sense is
heightened, every emotion is
magnified, our everyday reality is
shattered and we are flying into the
heavens. It may only last a moment,
an hour, an afternoon. But that doesn't
diminish its value. Because we are left
with memories that we treasure for the
rest of our lives

Why did you get divorced? He asked in
a commanding tone, I told him about
my ex husband's affair. "Well, my
divorce story is little different, my wife
refused to have a child, she wanted to
get into a management role before
pregnancy. I could not wait for so long,
especially that she used to come home

drunk after midnight." He said while checking his clock once more.

"I like you very much, will you marry me?" He pledged once again, this time looking like Jack Nicholson in "Psycho". "I feel very alone in this crowded world, I need someone to share my pain and joy with." He continued. His simplicity was attracting me, his verbosity was scaring me away. I said, "Since you are a very religious man, are your parent fine with an atheist bride?"

He takes his time for a few thoughts. The answer arouse on his face like roses in the morning. "Definitely, if you are Ok with me, I will share your number with my mother, you two can arrange for a meeting."

"Please go ahead" I nodded ironically.

Suddenly one alarm started ringing at 7:30 PM. Mr. Stampler almost jumped from his chair and told me "Sorry dear, I need to leave, got a client meeting at 8 PM, it was nice to meet you, can we meet again here tomorrow same time?" I gave him my most innocent smile "Yes!" I said softly.

Next day, we met again, I was there few minutes before the meeting, he was very happy that I came on time. I was wearing a blue long skirt, he praised, "You are looking more gorgeous today, and we will discuss something important that will make or break our relation." He took out a piece of paper and asked me, "What is your real age?" I took a deep breath and whispered him "32, why? He said, "I need to plan our marriage, child birth, child education, retirement for both of us."

"Are you being funny?" I asked in a frustrating tone. He wrote today's date in the paper and started scribbling marriage in next month, child by 2 years, and so on.
"After our child gets born, you have to quit your job and stay at home until the child starts schooling." He commanded. "That's really not necessary; so many new moms are working in our company, having their baby in children's corner where trained girls take good to the kids." I argued him.

Mr. Stampler whined "I do not want any housemaid to handle my child."

"Are there any more conditions?" I asked angrily. "Yes, you have to return home by 10 PM, no late night parties, I do not want your colleague, managers, and male friends to call you after 10 PM."

I thought of getting away from Mr. Stampler but could not find the proper reason... yet.

"One more thing, have you ever had any abortion?" he asked. I replied intrigued, "No, Why?"
"I do not want to marry such girl; abortion is against God's Holy work, it causes infection and reduces 'chance of pregnancy' significantly. It also increases chances for cancer, depression and suicide. I am marrying to make a family!"

NOW THAT WAS A PROPER REASON
FOR GETTING AWAY... BUT,
7:30 PM alarm came as a relief, the
same alarm as the evening before. He
just came out of the "Coffee Nights" for
the same reason: meeting with a
client.
His mom called me next morning, I
told her, "I cannot agree to the
conditions set by his son!"

MOTTO: Work out your own salvation.
Do not depend on others (Buddha).

One NRI Girl XI

Mr. Birch, a project manager working
in a large software service company
requested me for a dinner date.
We went for dinner at LA Nights
restaurant? Mr. Birch gave me a light

hug and tried to peck on my cheek; I stopped him and said, "I am not comfortable with this!" He carefully said, "Come on Sonja, this is how we greet each other in my Scandinavian society, you can be comfortable with such manners!" I kept quiet for some time. He indeed was a fine Swedish specimen, tall and bright blue eyes, with a floating blond hair. Just the right knight in shiny armor... or I thought so.

"I want to love you crazily Sonja, so much that you will go crazy without me," He said as we entered the long hallway of the restaurant, echoing with his expensive brown shoes hitting translucent floor. "Your lips is looking like a rose, I want to steal all the rosiness from them."
I got withdrawn to myself for unknown

reason. Maybe it was a shy and romantic tentative that I was looking for?

NOT BY FAR!

At dinner, Svensson Birch - as I later found the Scandinavian custom to full name your interlocutor, got drunk heavily and started letting out his secrets.

"Do you know how I screw the girls working in my company, who refuse to date me? I assign them work for which they do not have required skills, then client escalates the issue and I ask them to compromise or else I fire them." Now, that is so over with my romanticism!

He started whispering, "We, project managers gang up against fresher girls joining our company and ask them for a date".

AND THAT WAS MY DATE.

Or so he thought.... "If they refuse, we keep them in bench for a long time, else assign to a project which is in some third tier cities. We check their private chat logs and use it to coerce them for a date-to-force them sleeping with each one of us," Then I started to have my share of beers.

He continued, "For the girls who agrees to date but refuse to have sex, I give them bad performance rating at the end of the year, if they complain, I say, 'You did not perform at all, didn't you?'" He boasted while I was playing with my new I phone 6. I quipped, "But what about hard working girls, what if they refuse to date you?" trying to open up an evident grieving wound in his soul.

Mr. Birch gave me an evil smile and said, "I start tracking their "in and out time', 'lunch break', 'bathroom breaks' and so on! I read their private chat logs, then I give her list of policy violations. The girl gets scared and gives in, finally popping up in my bed."

"Do you take them to hotel or your house?" I asked.

"No, most of the restaurants/pubs have rooms which can be rented for an hour; I make good use of that time!"

"Whatever Mr. Svensson Birch, I am not interested," I walked away from the restaurant, or better said "pretended to..." as I slow down at half way to the door, hoping for him to stand by for a last chit-chat.

As I hoped for, he grabs my arm with a panted whisper in my ear, "You will

repent your behavior! how will you survive in the IT industry, my project manager gang is active in all IT companies!"
I DO NOT KNOW ABOUT ALL OF THE IT INDUSTRY, BUT I DO KNOW A LITTLE BIT ABOUT...SKYPE.

I said to him with a full smile of satisfaction.

Confused, he mechanically repeats: SKYPE? Do you work for them? - with a subdued voice. Poor guy did not get it yet.

NO DEAR, BUT OUR CHIT-CHAT IS LIVE ON SKYPE IN MY SKYPE GROUP.

Showing up my ongoing Skype as we talked the past half hour, he tried to cover his face and stumbled on his feet, still trying to digest the Skype shock. Thank you Skype, you saved me becoming a victim.

MOTTO: "Arrogance on the part of the meritorious is even more offensive to us than the arrogance of those without merit: for merit itself is offensive" - Friedrich Nietzsche.

Mr. Birch stopped being a bitch and I believe also stopped looking for a bitch, at least for a while.

One NRI Girl XII

I accepted interest from Mr. John, working as an Orthodox Priest and seeking to get a wife in order to get his parish.

We went out for a dinner.

John said, "Good evening Sonja, God has arranged for this meeting, I liked your profile very much and I am ready to marry you with the condition to baptize and accept the one true God.

"I do not believe in all these, I am a free bird, an atheist as you might be seeing in my profile." I told ruefully.

He quoted Einstein,
"The more I study science, the more I believe in God." and continued "Even the most illuminated scientific mind embraced God. Love comes from God, It's all written in the holy book, history proves Christianity as the one true and only religion" saying while visibly trying to convert me.

I asked, "Who wrote the Bible?" He replied, "The direct disciples of God, through the teachings of his Son."

I said ruefully, "You see John, I do not even trust what I watch in today's TV news or read in the newspapers, how can I trust a 2000 year old book?"

Priest John quoted Ralph Waldo Emerson,

"What lies behind us, and what lies before us are tiny matters compared to what lies within us."
He said with a lot of emotion, "You have to trust it and believe that our God sent his only and beloved Son to die for our sins and grant us forgiveness for all sins."

"If your God is so merciful, forgiving all type of sins for the believers, why cannot he become little more merciful and start forgiving sins of non believers, since not believing is less sinful than that of cheating, raping, murdering fellow human beings," I asked the intelligent question.

He replied in an offending tone, "Do not get into logical argument, God is beyond logic, you have to just trust Him to get eternal life! Love is God." And he quoted again, this time from Henry Ward Beecher: Of all the earthly music, that which reaches farthest into heaven, the beating of a truly loving heart is the finest."

And so I got the "evil" thought of tempting him. First I went to the toilet, making sure to walk slowly and confident. Behind me, I could sense the Priest's eyes watching me from behind like the beautiful witch from Snow White watch her mirror. When I got back from the toilet, I made myself sure that my generous breast got a little bit of freedom by opening my skirt too much.

I asked, "Will you give up your cross for me? I see you are blinded temporarily and suffering in solitude the whims while praying God, as religion blinded you with the cross." He suddenly got sober and exclaimed: "You had me take off my cross because it offended...."

I was expecting that sort of line. I've started to breath deep and turned my legs at the left side of the table - making sure he observe the fine line

from the top of my high heels to my
thin ankles and up the very tight and
short dress where my stockings were
ending. And so I interrupted him
rudely:
"It offended no one. No - it simply
appears to me to be discourteous to...
to wear the symbol of a deity long
dead. Our ancestors tried to find it.
And to open the door that separates us
from our Creator - whoever He might
be."
My Priest started to crumble, his face
get's reddish, his eyes share blinks
between down to my legs and up to
my face with sudden stops on my
pushed-up breasts. Quite shy he
stutters:

John: "But you need no doors to find
God.

If you believe...." Interrupting again is my favorite irritating technique, so I continued "Believe?! If you believe you are gullible. Can you look around this world and believe in the goodness of a God who rules it? Famine, Pestilence, War, Disease and Death! They rule this world."

Priest John:
"There is also love and beauty and hope. We are searching for these right now, don't we?"

"Very little hope I assure you. No. If a God of love and life and beauty ever did existed... he is long since dead. Someone... something else rules in his place. Believe? In a deity long dead? - I would rather be a pagan stumbled in rags and tatters while living my life to the fullest possibilities;"

JUST AS EXPECTED HE GOT
OFFENSIVE AND STARTED TO ARGUE
AGAINST MY BELIEFS.

"If atheists believe in nothing, then
why do they need a title? Doesn't that
believe in something? Something else
than God, making you split in
thousands of different false beliefs" He
insisted.
I replied, "But John, as per Wikipedia,
Christianity has got more than 5000
categories, each of them think only
they are true representative of the
God, rest will burn in hell - the same
as atheists like me. Also they do not
marry among each other; therefore
you WANT to convert me. You are
supposed to give 10% of whatever in
your wallet to the Church! For the past
thousand years, Vatican made money

by waiving off purgatory for people. Not to mention here the Inquisition, The Crusades, the Witch Hunt... Speaking of which, a few hundred years ago you would have burnt me alive for my beliefs. But Now you want to marry me?"

I continued, "There is no guarantee you will be saved, John!" and quoted Matthew 7:21: Not everyone who says to me, 'Lord, Lord,' will enter the kingdom of heaven, but only the one who does the will of my Father who is in heaven.

"John swiftly replies "Your quote is out of context."

I got irritated and told, "John, I have to leave now."

He grabbed my hand while I was
looking for my purse "Please don't
leave now. I want to do with you what
spring does with the cherry trees,
there is no need to worry, God
continuously forgives sins, so once you
start believing, you will be able to
enjoy his full love and kindness."

I watched him in his eyes and proudly
claimed my independence once again:
"I am never going to believe in that, if
God is so kind and forgive the sins of
all believers, I cannot forgive the
misery, death, child abuse, pestilence
and famine from our world." and
quipped, "Just leave me alone!"

The priest gave up and offered his last
gesture of kindness. "No problem, I
will drop you back to your home."

While dropping me back, John touched my leg few times while changing gear of the vehicle. I just folded my leg and stretched my elbow to avoid getting touched.

"Good night Sonja, God is waiting for you to come to His fold, call me any time you wish."

He preached to me for the last time. I did not bother to reply.

MOTTO:
"Religion is like a pair of shoes.... Find one that fits for you, but don't make me wear your shoes." -George Carlin.

One NRI Girl XIII

I accepted dating interest from Mr. Davis, a TV network director.

"I am currently working on a serial depicting various true rape events with enactment," he proclaimed.

I asked, "Is job of the producer about 'casting couch' and showing obscenity, violence in serials?"

He replied, "We do have rampant 'casting couches', we share details of the such girls and share them among us till they stay in the industry, if one girl is not ready to get laid, there are ten girls, who are ready to replace her for a small role, it is a "give and take" relationship, I do not see any harm in 'casting couch'. How would you pick one girl from thousand aspirants? Group sex reduces the resistance and shyness of the girl; she becomes more flexible on screen."

I gave my honest thoughts, "I guess that's the price for being famous".

He continued pleased, "We do show nudity, obscenity, violence, rape on screen, such scenes affects the soul and mind of the audience significantly, the more it affects the more profitable our serial becomes. We are in a cut throat business, if I do not show obscenity in my serial, someone else will, and public loves sex, violence and pornography. I will be thrown out of industry if my serials do not make profit."

Once we finished the dinner, he asked in a commanding tone, "I would like to spend whole night with you Honey."
On my refusal, he said, "I have put a spy camera under your seat and have already got your underwear

movements video recorded, if you do not oblige, I will upload it on a porn site and tell people to contact me to know the name of the girl who performed in this video."

I said, "You will land in jail, it is punishable offence to upload private videos to Internet." He said, "Since face is not visible, you will not be able to prove that in court, but I will share this video with your friends and colleagues and inform them that it is Sonja's video, if you want me to delete the video, at least you have to suck my dry." He commanded. "I rather prefer to die." I told him.

"Sonja, do not shout, let's get into a room, I have rented one for the whole night, it is in your interest only, you would not want this video to be uploaded in a porn site," he whispered.

He grabbed my hand and dragged me into the room, I followed him reluctantly. "Please delete my video and let me go, you will land in jail,i" I screamed inside the room.

"Sonja, last month, your brother had sex with one of the girl working under me, he performed like animal, I have got that video, and do you want to watch the video? I can get your brother in jail for a long time in rape charges,i" he told in an authoritative tone.

I screamed, "What do you want from me?i"
He replied, "I want you to cooperate with me. I will satisfy my lust on you and let you go." Then he threw me on bed and overpowered to take away my tops, I was left wearing bra and skirt,

he then tried to take out my skirt, I turned over and could land a kick on him.

"I am not going to rape you, calm down Sonja, let's just do oral, I will delete the video and let you go, no one will ever know about it," he told in a soft tone.

I thought of cooperating with him and told, "I can use my hand," he agreed, I started shaking him, 10 minutes passed by, suddenly, he tried to grab me by hair and tried to ejaculated on my face, I could escape that, he ejaculated it on my top and cleaned himself, he then grabbed me and bit my lip. That hurt.

He ordered me to wear the top back, he again grabbed me from behind and squeezed my breasts and I used my perse to hit him in the chest. He released me and deleted the video. He dropped me at my home and said, "Sonja, let's keep today's event between us, if you ever want to act in a TV serial or movie, just ask me, I will arrange and fix up with the producer and director, in exchange you have to really sleep with couple of guys."

I did not know, how I would have returned home with a smelly top in the bus.

MOTTO:
"Beauty provokes harassment, the law says, but it looks through men's eyes when deciding what provokes it."
Naomi Wolf.

One NRI Girl XIV

I accepted marriage proposal from Mr.
Collins.

He claimed that he had dated more
than 500 girls in Boston and had sex
with more than 250 of them, girls find
him irresistible. Any girl who refuses to
have sex with him, he blacklists the
girl and informs his friend's circle about
her. He also exchanges information
about "girls who jump to bed at very
first datei" with his friends.

He boasted about not using condom
while having sex, he claimed, "I carry
a spy pen camera to record each of my
sexual acts and keep this as a souvenir
cum guarantee that the girl will not file

a rape case against me after few months.i"

"I have made minimum 100 girls pregnant, only mogul emperors can boast this kind of record." he joked.

He said, "I get attracted to girls like a dog, I spend 50% of my salary every month to get dates and get laid. Each time, I could sleep with a new girl, I feel like scoring a goal. However, I do avoid sleeping with same girl more than 5 times."

I asked, "Why do you want to get married now? You are having more sex than that of married guys!" He replied, "Good question, I am getting old, getting new girls is becoming more difficult, I am having some difficulties in having sex now, my tool itches a lot at the time when having sex. I want to start saving money for future, sometime I feel like a sex addicted dog, I want love and affection more than sex now, but no girl gives me that, they are interested in my money and my body."

I told him, "Neither I am looking to marry any sex addict nor I want to get STD."

"Ok, I will drop you back to your home," he told in a sad voice.

Suddenly he stopped his car in a dark zone; he grabbed my hair using one hand and put the other hand inside my skirt. He started rubbing my underwear vigorously. I used my elbow to hit him, he started abusing me, "You bitch, I have spent 500$ for your transport, gift and dinner, and you have to give me something in return.i"

I shouted for help and suddenly a bike with two passengers stopped near the car and directed the bike's head light into the car, Collins got scared and let me go, I straightened my hairs and came out of the car, before the bike riders could question him, he escaped in his car.

MOTTO: "Every form of addiction is bad, no matter whether the narcotic, alcohol, morphine or fantasies." - C.G. Jung.

One NRI Girl XV

Mr. Mohan, a Hindu civil engineer, called me and told, "I would like to meet you tomorrow, and here is an innovative plan for our date as. Can we take a cab from your home to the airport and back, that way, we get two hours of private time. If you do not like, you can drop off the cab any time." I called Michelle, she told me to keep a pepper spray in my bag.

I got a call at 7 PM from Mr. Spiritual that he was waiting outside my apartment. I found a smiling, medium built, quite fair person, I got into the the taxi with him. He greets me, gentle caressing my hand.

"Sonja, I am very happy to meet you." he said.

His hand was smoother than mine; his eyes were quite calm and attractive. I got somewhat excited when he touched my hand. We two seem to be a good match physically.

As told by Michelle, I took phone number of the driver and send an SMS to Michelle with it.

We sat closely and I remember that a sudden car bump throw him little bit and his upper arm touched mine in an unexpected way. His arm was cooler than mine. I liked it and thought of awarding Mr. Roland and kiss on his cheek.

He recited a Hindu poetry written by some saint named Kabir:

"THE flute of the Infinite is played without ceasing,
Its sound is love.
When love renounces all limits,

It reaches truth.

How widely the fragrance spreads,

It has no end.

Nothing stands in its way.

The form of this melody is bright like a

million suns.

"All these are old and outdated

concept, too deep for my taste." I tried

to change the topic.

He then quoted Shakespeare,

"My love as deep; the more I give to

thee,

The more I have, both are infinite."

He continued,

"You now understand that love is a

subtle form of energy which can

extend from one end to the other end of the Universe,"
I was impressed he started our date with a NOT INTERESTED IN SEX approach. "You seem to be quite different from all the guys, I dated, they just want to talk about sex and get me into their bed quickly," I said.

Mr Mohan: "It all depends on the level of consciousness, like if you ask a dog, whether consent needs to be taken before sex, it will say no, if you ask a porn star about rape, she may say, 'rape is just sex by surprise', if you ask a porn addict, whether watching violent rape scenes affect him? He will say, no, but it has been scientifically proved that watching movies, videos, etc. affects our brain in a significant way," He continued,

"What is the solution to this problem?"
I interrupted him.

He answered immediately, "There is
one very good prayer in RigVeda,"

Om, Lead us from Unreality to the
Reality
Lead us from the Darkness to the Light
Lead us from Death to Immortality.
Om Peace, Peace, Peace.

"Life is a God given opportunity for us
to go from darkness to light," he
explained,

I found his statements very funny but
with a good logic within. "Let me ask
him few tricky questions," I thought.

I asked, "Who created God?"

Mr. Roland replied, "Energy cannot be created or destroyed, you may think God as an all pervasive subtle form of energy."

He recited Saint Kabir again,

"He who has seen that radiance of love, he is saved."

Completely unsatisfied by his answer I made sure he gets my.... spiritual energy.

"Shall we meet again?" he asked.

I told him, "I am sorry. But you do not seem to be a good match for marriage; I would like you to be a good friend."

Mohan joyfully said, "Fine, I respect your wish!"

Suddenly full moon came out from the veil of cloud and looked at us through the car windows.
"It is full moon today, I love the light of full moon," he smiled.

Mohan dropped me to my house after two hours of tensed drive and said, "Good night, please keep in touch, I do not have any hard feeling about the rejection!" I said, "We can be good friends."

Motto: "It is not more surprising to be born twice than once; everything in nature is resurrection." —Voltaire

One NRI Girl XVI

Mr. Sherman, a state level cricketer from India, a well built guy bathed in good perfume picked me up for lunch at 2 PM. He shook my hand for a long time and tried to tickle it. I took my hand away.

He started the conversation, "Sonja, I am a hard-core cricketer and have scored more than thousands runs in first class cricket, which of all sports do you like?"

I said, "Swimming, table tennis."
He smiled and asked, "Do you know, what the best sport in world is?"

I said, "I guess, it is swimming."

He replied fast, "No sweet girl, sex is the best sports in the world, men and women are playing every day but they never get retired. See, we cricketer plays the game for 10-15 years and retire, you software folks may retire in 15-20 years, but people continue to play sex sports till they die. Do you understand?"

He continued, "Will you be able to pay me USD 100,000 loan after marriage? I need to bribe it to get chance in test team, once I get into the team; I will be able to recover the money in few months."

I said, "You want 100k dowry?" He replied, "No, I will repay you once I play test cricket."

He continued, "Sonja, do you know, many girls just die to have sex with a cricketer, after the match is over, many girls flock to the club/hotel where cricketers spend time, some openly ask for sexual favor from the cricketers, many cricketers get trapped by bookies after taking sex drugs they lose conscience and perform sex like animal. Such acts are video recorded and then bookie continues to blackmail those cricketers for various information, they even force cricketers to sell games, drop catch. Given a choice, which cricketer would you like to have sex?"

I told him, "Can we change topic? I am not comfortable discussing about all these." "Then, I can teach you how to play cricket," He quipped.

"That will be awesome," I replied.

"Do you prefer indoor cricket or outdoor, I prefer indoor cricket, God has given us bat and ball, we can make good use of them," he chuckled.

"Outdoor cricket," I diverted his topic. He took me to nearby playing ground where a team was already playing; he introduced himself and got both of us included in fielding team. He started throwing the ball aiming my breast any time he fielded the ball, "Sonja, catch it," I could manage to catch first two, third one hit my breast, I got hurt, Mr. Sherman came running, and started massaging the affected area, he started touching even the other breast, I asked him to stop. He brought a spray and sprayed it aiming it at my nipple; I screamed at him and got out of the field. I took a cab and returned to my flat, it took many months for the

pain and the regrets for this date to
subside.

MOTTO: "Maybe all one can do is hope
to end up with the right regrets." -
Arthur Miller.

One NRI Girl XVII

Mr. Martins, marketing professional
took me to a very costly restaurant;
spend around $250 only for dinner.

He proclaimed, "Sonja, I am a
teetotaler, if you would like to have
drink, please feel free to order, I will
not restrict your freedom."

He continued, "What is the most
beautiful thing in world?" I replied,
"Water fountain?"

"No, it is love," he quoted Helen Keller,

The best and most beautiful things in
this world cannot be seen or even
heard, but must be felt with the heart.

I was very impressed with his soberness. While returning, he asked me for a kiss. I obliged.

He grabbed me completely and kissed me few times and then said, "Thank you, Sonja."

He said, "Next weekend, can we go for swimming together? I have a club membership.i" I agreed.

The next Saturday we reached at swimming pool at around 8PM, Both of us changed to swimming dress and jumped into a huge swimming pool, after few minutes, we saw, other couples in compromising positions inside swimming pool. He said, "Sonja, let's swim together.i" We swam away from public view and then suddenly, he grabbed me from behind and started caressing my abdomen, side of abdomen and arm pit, I tried to release myself, he pressed my breasts. I used my arm and hit him in his solar plexus, he lost grip on me, I released myself from his clutches and came out of the swimming pool. He followed me and begged for forgiveness, telling me, "I love you Sonja, Please forgive me. I could not control myself. You were looking so hot in swimming suit, I thought, you would be willing to have sex like the other swimming pool couples we've seen."

His sudden caressing had excited me sexually, so I decided to forgive him. He again asked for a kiss, I obliged, he grabbed me like a bear and kissed with passion. I again pushed him back when I felt is too much.

Next weekend, we decided to go for a late night movie. It was a "Love & Romance" type of movie, every time the hero was grabbing heroine, Mr Martins was grabbing me and kissing my cheek. When the hero grabbed his heroine and kissed her,
Martins grabbed and kissed me also, he then started groping me and I slapped him.

In the movie hall, I saw many couple in obscene positions. Then there was a rape scene in the movie, Martins put his leg on top of my leg and grabbed me from side, he started rubbing his leg on my leg, suddenly, he tried to put his hand inside my skirt, I shouted, "Stop." He replied calmly, "Ok, darling." For the rest of the movie, he did not disturb me. He dropped me at my flat without any hassles and bade me good night.

Next morning, Martins called me and said, "I want to marry you in a temple." He seems to be in love with me, I love the way he hugs me, grabs me and kisses me, except his pushiness.

I agreed to his proposal.
He said, "Let's go to a Las Vegas resort, next weekend, I will book separate rooms, we can spend lot of time together.i"

This is a golden opportunity, I had not have sex for a long time, Martins seems to be madly in love with me.

I called Michelle and asked, "I am going to Las Vegas next weekend and do you think is wise to have sex with Mr Martins? She suggested, "It is Ok to have sex, just ensure that lights are off so that he cannot video record the act. Make him wear condom even before foreplay."

He drove me to Las Vegas, I came to know that he had booked only one room for both of us as I have expected; he had put my name as Ms. Martins. I got totally angry with his tricks.

I said, "Please cancel the booking and let's go back to Boston immediately." he told, "Roads are not safe at night, few girls got waylaid and raped in last few months."

He knelt down in front of me, holding a gold ring and asked me, "|Sonja, I love you, will you marry me?" "How cute! Yes!" I said. He put the gold ring on my finger.

We decided to spend the night together, after closing the door of the room, he gave me a tight hug, started sucking my lip. Then he started undressing me, I objected slightly, he then started sucking my left breast, and cuddling the other breast.
He reached for my underwear, I hold it tight, he started rubbing my private parts vigorously, I lost control and gave in. He quickly took out underwear, I was lying naked, he started licking my private part like a mad dog and I was ready for sex after many months. He pounced upon me and had sex for almost ten minutes, he was not using any protection, I came back to my sense, I tried to take him

out, he overpowered me and continued to enjoy my body for few more minutes and then he came inside me.

I went to bath room and washed myself clean. We slept together whole night, at dawn, he again asked for sex, I was in no mood for it, but he forcefully made it.

It hurt my body and soul. Since he promised to marry me within few weeks, I took it lightly.

After coming back from Las Vegas, Martins stopped picking up my calls. I came to know from one of his friend that, "He is going to marry someone from his company and that it is a financial marriage." I called him, he told that, "He talked to his parents about me, they said, they will never accept anyone from the middle society as daughter in law, I am sorry, Sonja, I cannot marry you, please forgive me."

Later, I came to know, that this guy has cheated dozens of girls like me, "He takes them to a resort, gives gold ring, and sleep with them with promise of marriage."

I thought of taking some action against this cheater. I called up human resource department of his company and told them, that their employee has cheated me, and requested them to take action against Martins. HR asked me to file a FIR and submit a copy of the FIR to the company.

I went to police station to file a complaint about this guy, but the police laughed at my story saying that I had dated the guy multiple times; I consensually had sex with him, knowing very well that there was hardly any chance of marriage!

One policeman quipped, "If people get milk for free, why will they buy cow? It is your fault, nowadays everybody is sleeping with everybody else, and it is not our job to keep a track on this." Another policewoman told, "If I spend night with a guy in same room, will he worship me at night?"

I came back from police station empty handed. The HR informed Mr Martins about my complaint and asked him to file a counter complaint against me, which he did, not before going to the police station and bribe someone to make the entry in police register as,

"Ms, Sonja is harassing him for marriage for the past few months."

Martins then thought he should teach me a lesson for complaining to his company.

One evening, he came to my flat, when I opened my door, he immediately grabbed me by hair and told, "Bitch, why did you complain to my company? If I lose job, you will be gang raped by my friends."

I asked him to leave my apartment immediately, he slapped me, I started shouting for help, no one came, he tried to kiss me forcefully, I pushed him hard, then one old woman with walking stick came out her flat and saw us, she asked Martins to leave me but he even abused that old lady and asked her not to meddle in his private affairs. The old woman called two more old women who were her morning walk partners.

Martins tried to take out my shirt, then the three old women came to my defense and one of them hit him hard with her walking stick. Suddenly Martins left me and in the mean time, our apartment security guards came and grabbed Martins from behind, tied him to the exit gate. Police arrived one hour later and Mr. Martins immediately told police, "Sonja was harassing me for marriage and I have come to request her to stop it. I have already complained about her in my police station; please have a look at the receipt of complaint." The policemen asked the old women and the security guards about the incident. They got convinced that Martins was the culprit. They took him to police station and took a written undertaking that, "He will not come anywhere near to me or else he will be liable for prosecution."

I thanked the old women and security folks from bottom of my heart, if they would not have come to my help on time, I would have been raped or killed.

I decided to stop dating these animals in men's clothing.

MOTTO: "The best things come to those who wait." - Marilyn Grey.

About Author

Rupi Kaur is author of bestselling book, "One NRI Girl". She writes in Romance, Women Issues and Humor niche.

CPSIA information can be obtained
at www.ICGtesting.com
Printed in the USA
LVHW041916241118
598131LV00026B/620/P